ANGUS
and the
Mona Lisa

Story and Pictures
by Jacqueline Cooper

Lothrop, Lee & Shepard Books · New York

Copyright © 1981 by Jacqueline Cooper
All rights reserved. No part of this book may be reproduced or utilized in any form or by any means, electronic or mechanical, including photocopying, recording or by any information storage and retrieval system, without permission in writing from the Publisher. Inquiries should be addressed to Lothrop, Lee & Shepard Books, a division of William Morrow & Company, Inc., 105 Madison Avenue, New York, New York 10016. Printed in the United States of America. First Edition.
1 2 3 4 5 6 7 8 9 10

Library of Congress Cataloging in Publication Data
Cooper, Jacqueline   Angus and the Mona Lisa.
Summary: Angus the cat helps thwart the theft of the famous Mona Lisa.   [1. Art thefts—Fiction.   2. Cats—Fiction.   3. Mystery and detective stories]   I. Title.
PZ7.C7858An   [E]   80-13506
ISBN 0-688-41972-0   ISBN 0-688-51972-5 (lib. bdg.)

For Yasmine and Henri Dubois-Ferrière

"We're all going to Paris," Carol said to Angus one day. "To find out about our French ancestors."

Angus purred. He had French roots himself. He was descended from Chat Pierre, who had come from France to fight alongside General Washington at Valley Forge. Angus also had a distant cousin, Émile, living on Cat Street in Paris.

Carol bought a special pet carrier for Angus so that she could keep him with her on the plane.

But when they got to the airport the ticket agent said, "Sorry. Only one pet is allowed in the cabin, and we already have a dog on board."

And before you could say "crêpes Suzette," Angus was in the baggage compartment and the plane was flying over the Atlantic Ocean.

Fancy doing this to a *cat!*" said Angus. It was pitch black all around him. "I hope that dog barks all the way to Paris," Angus said out loud to no one. Then Angus heard something that made his hair stand up.

A deep voice said, "Are you all right, Turtle Dove?" Angus saw a man sitting up in a trunk and holding a flashlight.

As Angus watched in the dim light, the man opened a second trunk. A thin, dark-haired woman sat up inside it. "It won't be long now," said the man.

The woman said, *"Agri."*

Agri must mean "yes" in some foreign language, Angus thought.

"And then we will have the Mona Lisa, and we will be rich!" the man said.

"Agri," the woman said again.

The Mona Lisa! One of the most famous paintings in the world! It was hanging in the Louvre, a museum in Paris. There was a picture of it in one of Carol's books. Angus had thought the Mona Lisa's smile was very much like his own — a little mysterious.

I must find a way to stop these thieves! he thought. Quickly, he undid the latch of his carrier and stepped out. Angus hid between two suitcases and listened to the man and woman talk. He learned that the man's name was Pigeon, and that he and Turtle Dove were to meet someone called the Baron in the wine cellar of a café on the corner of the *rue des Chats.*

When they felt the plane begin its descent, Pigeon and Turtle Dove got back into their trunks and closed the lids. It was dark again. Angus silently crept close to the trunks and waited.

When the plane landed at Charles de Gaulle airport, it was morning. A baggage handler came into the hold and put the trunks on a cart. Angus heard him whisper to the trunks.

"Everything has been arranged. You are diplomatic baggage and will not be inspected. The Baron awaits you at the café. *Agri.*"

He wheeled the trunks to a small van and put them inside. Angus jumped in too. No one saw him.

When they reached the café, Angus followed the trunks
into the wine cellar where the Baron waited.

The trunks were opened and out came Turtle Dove
and Pigeon.

"*Agri, agri,*" said the Baron. "I have been expecting you. *Agri. A-a-a*—achoo!" Suddenly he began to sneeze and sneeze and *sneeze!* Then he saw Angus.

"Don't you know I'm allergic to cats, you fools?" he roared.

The Baron's bodyguards kicked Angus into a closet and locked the door.

That hurt! Angus was about to put up a howling protest when he heard the Baron say, "Tonight … the Louvre … *agri* …"

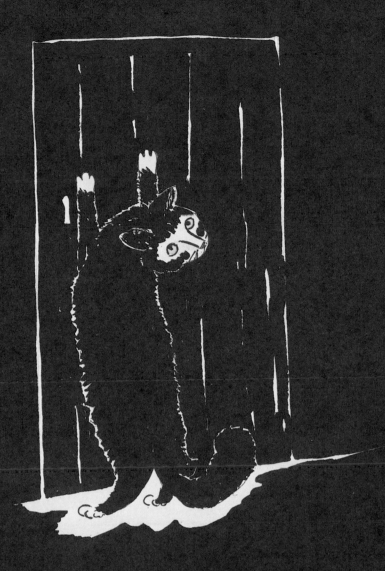

Tonight! Angus had to get out somehow. He must save the
Mona Lisa! The back wall of the closet was made of dirt.
Angus scratched and dug, and dug and scratched. He had
thought of a plan, but he would need help.

Just as he was beginning to think he could not dig any
longer, he saw daylight.

He crawled out, dusty and tired, and blinked in the
bright sunlight.

The street, with French flags draped across it, had a
holiday look.

Then Angus remembered that the next day would be the Fourteenth of July, France's Independence Day. He began to clean himself. Then he noticed that the street was full of cats. It was Cat Street!

"*Excusez-moi*," he said politely to a tiger cat who was enjoying a dish of filet of sole. "I am a stranger in your beautiful city. Do you know where I can find my cousin, Émile? He's a big orange tabby."

The tiger cat looked him over and replied, "Émile works nights at the Wine-Taster's Café. He's asleep now. Would you like to meet his sister, Antoinette, instead?"

"*Oui*," said Angus in his best French. "There is no time to lose!"

Angus discovered that Antoinette was not only a very smart cat, she also worked for Interpol. When she heard his story she said, "We must not allow the Mona Lisa to be stolen! Tell me your plan."

"*Bon*!" said Angus. "This is what I think we should do."

That night, Angus led an elite cat squad to the Louvre.
Cousin Antoinette met him in the courtyard where another
cat squad waited under her command.

"The thieves will enter at midnight," whispered Angus. He
hoped his plan would work.

Angus led his squad inside. They took up positions in the gallery where the Mona Lisa hung.

At midnight the door opened slowly and someone dressed as a gendarme tiptoed in.

"Gendarmes don't tiptoe!" whispered Angus. "That's Pigeon dressed as a gendarme, and here comes Turtle Dove disguised as a cleaning woman!"

Pigeon and Turtle Dove went straight to the painting and lifted it from its place on the wall. They wrapped it in a cloth and then put it in a linen bag. Angus wondered whether the Mona Lisa was still smiling inside the bag.

When the thieves started to tiptoe out, Angus gave the signal to attack.

Antoinette and her group rushed at Pigeon and Turtle Dove from the courtyard, while Angus and his squad dropped down on them from above. It was a beautiful operation.

The Baron was watching from a balcony across the street. When he saw all the cats, he jumped down and tried to escape. But Antoinette and her squad caught up with him before he got to the corner.

With so many cats all around him, the Baron's allergy took a nasty turn. He sneezed and sneezed and broke out in a hideous rash. He sneezed so much he couldn't move. He was still sneezing when the French police came and arrested everyone.

At noon that day during the Independence Day celebrations,
Angus was decorated for his bravery and his service to
France. Then, with Cousin Antoinette, he led the Cat Parade
down the beautiful Champs Élysées.

Carol and her mother and father saw the whole story of Angus and the Mona Lisa on the TV news. They had been very worried about Angus. They were overjoyed to know that Angus was not only alive and well and in Paris, but he was also a very smart cat—which was, of course, something Carol had suspected all along.

Jacqueline Cooper was born in Alexandria, Egypt, but is now an American citizen. She lives in Washington, D.C., where she is well known for her watercolors of French streets, which she fills with her whimsical cats. She travels several times a year to visit her married daughter, a physician in a London hospital, or her niece and nephew who live in Switzerland, and to whom this book is dedicated. *Cocktails and Camels,* her earlier book, was for adults; *Angus and the Mona Lisa* is her first children's book.

Jacqueline Cooper loves animals, and once flew to Paris with her real cat, Angus. She says, "Angus traveled in a container with the top down, sitting on the seat next to mine, eating shrimp."